Max Mouse is always looking for adventure. He is lively and full of exciting ideas.

D1588198

Joe Crow runs the airport in Fabuland. He is a fearless pilot, always ready to try out new daredevil flying stunts.

Wilfred Walrus is captain of the ferry, and loves to tell stories of life at sea.

Lionel Lion is the mayor of Fabuland. He feels very important as he drives round in his big shiny car.

written by
Michael Cole

**Have you heard of Fabuland?
It's not far away – just a little to
the left as you go north, or a little
to the right as you go south.**

**Edward Elephant lives there,
and so do all his friends. Read about their
exciting adventures in this series.**

Acknowledgment
Film stills by FilmFair

British Library Cataloguing in Publication Data

Cole, Michael, *1933-*
    Lionel's party: Edward and the camera.—(LEGO Group).
    I. Title
    823'.914 [J]   PZ7
    ISBN 0-7214-1063-4

First edition

Published by Ladybird Books Ltd Loughborough Leicestershire UK
Ladybird Books Inc Lewiston Maine 04240 USA

® The LEGO logo and FABULAND are registered trademarks belonging to the LEGO Group.
© LEGO GROUP MCMLXXXVII
© LADYBIRD BOOKS LTD MCMLXXXVII
*All rights reserved. No part of this publication may be reproduced, stored in a retrieval
system, or transmitted in any form or by any means, electronic, mechanical, photo-copying,
recording or otherwise, without the prior consent of the copyright owners.*

Printed in England

Lionel's party

Ladybird Books

Lionel's party

Lionel Lion, mayor of Fabuland, had invited all his friends to a fancy dress party.

All the invitations had been delivered and everyone was very excited – there was going to be a competition for the best fancy dress costume.

"I'll go as a car," said Max. He found an old cardboard box and painted some wheels on the sides. He put it over his head and soon he was driving and hooting round the room.

Bonnie and Edward thought and thought, but they couldn't decide.

"I could go as a clown...no, not unusual enough," said Edward. "Or a pirate?"

"I could go as a princess...no, too ordinary," said Bonnie. "Or a nurse?"

They paced up and down but still couldn't think of anything.

"I'll just have to go as a bunny," sighed Bonnie.

"But you are one already, just like I'm an elephant," replied Edward. "You can't go to a fancy dress party dressed as yourself."

"Wait a minute, I have an idea!" said Bonnie. "If I can't go as me," she whispered to Edward, "I could go as *you* – dressed as an elephant!"

"That certainly would be unusual!" said Edward. "But what about me? What can I go as? I can think of nothing."

"Well, what about going as *nothing*?" laughed Bonnie. "You could go as the Invisible Elephant!"

"What a terrific idea!" said Edward. "I just can't wait to see Lionel Lion's face when he sees me – or doesn't, as the case may be." And Edward and Bonnie set to work to make their costumes.

The day of the fancy dress party
arrived. It was sunny and warm,
and Lionel Lion, dressed as a
magnificent magician, stood in the
Town Hall garden to say hello to
his guests.

The first was Boris Bulldog, who
came dressed as a clown.

"You make a very good clown," said Lionel. "You're almost as good a clown as you are a postman!"

"Watch this!" said Boris, and he started to juggle with some balls. "See how many I can keep up in the air at the same time."

Up they went, and down they came again, all over the place, as Max, pretending to be a car, bumped into Boris and knocked the balls out of his hand.

"You've ruined my act!" said Boris, crossly.

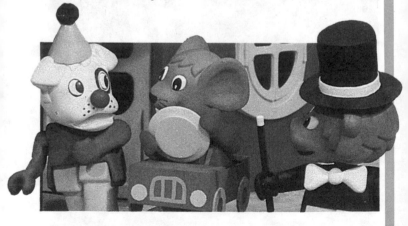

"Sorry, beep, Boris," said Max. "Very, beep beep, sorry!" And off he went, hooting round the garden.

Wilfred Walrus came dressed as a pirate. "Ha, ha," he cried. "Sixty silver sovereigns submerged in seaweed."

Suddenly, a loud cackling laugh rang out. Hannah Hippopotamus, dressed as a witch, zoomed onto the lawn as if she were flying on a broomstick.

"Oh, very good, Hannah. That *was* a surprise, I must say," said Lionel.

"Which is more than I can say for you, young Edward," he said, turning to Bonnie, who was wearing a trunk to look like Edward.

"Wait a minute. That's not Edward!" said Lionel, looking very closely at the elephant.
"It's *you*, Bonnie! You looked just like Edward. But where is he?"

"Here," said a voice
that sounded like Edward's.

Lionel looked round,
but he could see no sign
of the elephant.

"Where?" he asked.

"Here," said Edward's
voice. Lionel turned round.
The voice seemed to be
coming from a tree on the lawn.

"I'm the Invisible Elephant," it said.

"There's no such thing," said Lionel.

"Isn't there?" said Edward, and a branch of the tree moved and tapped Lionel on the shoulder.

17

"My word, Edward," said Lionel. "You certainly fooled me. It's *tree*-mendous! Now, come on. Let's all have some party cake."

Lionel led the way to the table and gave everyone a big piece of chocolate cake. But when it came to Edward's turn, all the cake had gone.

"What's happened to the cake?" said Edward, looking at the empty plate.

"Here's your piece," said Lionel, tapping the plate.

"But there's nothing there," said Edward.

"Of course not," said Lionel. "It's like you...invisible!"

With an *abra-ca-da-bra* Lionel produced a piece of cake by magic, just for Edward! Then he picked up a big red rosette and fastened it to Edward's trunk.

"I'm proud to present you with first prize," he said. And everyone clapped and cheered.

Edward and
the camera

Edward was helping Wilfred
Walrus to clear out his store room,
when they found a large camera.

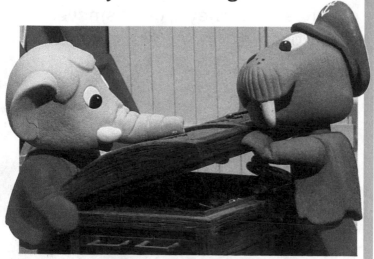

 "My old camera!"
said Wilfred. "I
haven't seen that
for years." He
picked up the
camera.

"You know, young Edward," said Wilfred, "that camera has been with me round the world and back again on my sea journeys, but it's never taken pictures of my own country, Fabuland."

"Well, it's not too late," said Edward. "I can take some pictures for you and put them in a special book."

"Good idea," said Wilfred, and he showed Edward how to use the camera. They loaded it with film, and Wilfred wished Edward good luck as he set off to take his first picture.

Hannah Hippopotamus was singing to her flowers (as she always did – to make them grow) when Edward passed by.

He thought that a picture of Hannah in her garden would be very good for Wilfred's book, so he asked her to stand by her flowers.

"Smile, please, Hannah!" said Edward. "Say 'cheese!'"

"Cheese!" she said.

"Thanks, Hannah," said Edward, and he hurried off to take a photograph of his friends, Bonnie Bunny and Max Mouse.

Edward found Bonnie sitting in her chair at home. "Come on, Bonnie," said Edward. "Smile, please." But Bonnie wasn't in the mood for smiling.

Then Max had an idea. He tiptoed behind Edward and the camera, stood on his head and giggled. And soon Bonnie couldn't help laughing.

"That's good, Bonnie!" said Edward as he took the picture.

Edward took another picture of Max, still upside down. "Got you!" he said, feeling very pleased.

"But I'm upside down," said Max.

"Well," said Edward, "I'll put this picture upside down in the book, and then it will look the right way up — if you see what I mean."

Just then a car
hooter sounded
and Lionel Lion,
mayor of Fabuland,
drove up. Edward
rushed out.

"Excuse me, Mr Mayor," he said. "I'd like to take a picture of you in your car. Would you smile for me, please?"

"Of course I will," said Lionel proudly. He made himself look as important as he could.

Edward took the picture and thanked him, then he walked on to Catherine Cat's restaurant.

Billy and Freddy were sitting outside. He was just about to take a photograph of them, when Clive Crocodile stepped in front of the camera.

"Can I be in the photograph, too?" asked Clive.

"Certainly, Clive... with the others," replied Edward.

"Will here do?" said Clive, standing in front of everyone.

"I can't see anything but a green crocodile," said Edward, peering through the camera lens. "You'll have to move, Clive."

"Oh, sorry," said Clive and he stepped back to join the others.

At last they were ready, and Edward took a picture of everyone together.

"That will be a good one for Wilfred's book," he said. "Ah, that reminds me, I must get a picture of Wilfred."

Edward went down to the
harbour to find Wilfred.

"I'd like to take a picture of you
please, Wilfred — with the ferry in
the background," said Edward.

Wilfred walked to the water's edge. With the ferry behind him, he turned round to face Edward.

"Back a bit," said Edward, pointing the camera at Wilfred. "A bit more, please."

"No, stop!" cried Bonnie, rushing up. "You'll fall in the water, Wilfred. Don't look round."

"Don't look...oh!" said Wilfred as he spun round and landed safely on the quayside.

"That was a close thing," he gasped.

Edward snapped the picture. "Now I've got a picture of everyone," he said happily.

Wilfred sat down to look at Edward's pictures, and everyone crowded round.

"What's that fuzzy thing?" said Wilfred, pointing to the photographs.

And there, in every picture, was a very strange black shape.

Then Bonnie suddenly began to laugh.

"What's so funny?" asked Edward.

"It's your trunk, Edward," said Bonnie. "It must have got in front of the camera. It's come out in every picture!"

"Oh, no," said Edward. "I'm sorry!"

"Never mind," said Wilfred. "Now that everyone is here, you can take a photograph of all of us together."

Bonnie tied a balloon to Edward's trunk to keep it out of the way of the camera.

"Hold it! Smile, please," said Edward. "Say 'cheese!'"

"Cheese!" they said, and Edward took a picture. He didn't mind not being in it himself because, after all, he *was* in all the others – or, at least, one part of him was.

Freddy Fox enjoys running the General Store, and always has lots of bargains.

Mike Monkey spends most of his time with Wilfred on the ferry, although he should be helping Billy Bear to run the service station.

Poor Clive Crocodile is rather foolish and clumsy and he often spoils things for the others.

Billy Bear likes inventing things – but they don't always work out the way he intends.